For Claudia —L.P.
For Hanspeter —K.S.

Lorenz Pauli and Kathrin Schärer created this picture book in cooperation with the Swiss Association of the general public libraries SAB.

Copyright © 2011 by Atlantis, an imprint of Orell Füssli Verlag AG, Zürich, Switzerland.
Original edition published in German under the title *Pippilothek??? Eine Bibliothek wirkt Wunder*.
English translation copyright © 2013 by NorthSouth Books Inc., New York 10016.
Translated by Andrew Rushton.

First published in the United States, Great Britain, Canada, Australia, and New Zealand in 2013 by NorthSouth Books Inc., an imprint of NordSüd Verlag AG, CH-8005 Zürich, Switzerland.

Distributed in the United States by NorthSouth Books Inc., New York 10016.
Library of Congress Cataloging-in-Publication Data is available.

ISBN: 978-0-7358-4150-5
Printed in Germany by Grafisches Centrum Cuno GmbH & Co. KG, 39240 Calbe, June 2013.
1 3 5 7 9 • 10 8 6 4 2

www.northsouth.com

MIX
Paper from responsible sources
FSC
www.fsc.org
FSC® C043106

The Fox in the Library

Lorenz Pauli • Kathrin Schärer

Mouse was enjoying some peace
and quiet, when all at once she smelled
a fox. Then she heard a noise....

North South

"Now, I've got you!" growled Fox.

But Mouse disappeared through a cellar window.

"Wait!" Fox snarled, chasing after her—down into the cellar, over a box, around a corner, and into a pipe.

At last Fox squeezed himself out of the tight spot.

"Where's that Mouse!" he growled and snuffled. But all he could smell was paper . . . and people.

"There you are!" he shouted.

Mouse scurried behind some shelves, and Fox dashed after her.

Suddenly Mouse stopped in her tracks. "Hey! This is a very special place—a place where you shouldn't annoy others. And you are being *REALLY* annoying!"

"I'm going to grab you; you're mine!" growled Fox.

"Nothing here belongs to you," Mouse said with a giggle. "You can only *borrow* things here. And I'll never be yours. This isn't the forest; this is the library."

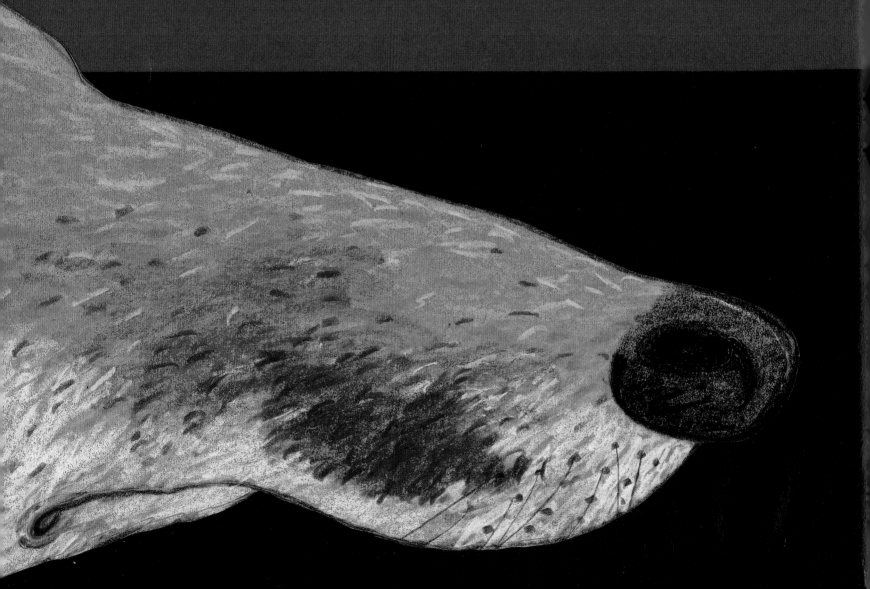

"A lie-what?" asked Fox.

"A library," said Mouse.

Fox looked around and said, "What's a lie-berry?"

"A library is a place full of books to read and borrow. You need books to have adventures . . . and to learn new things . . . and to have new ideas," said Mouse.

Then she picked out a picture book from the shelf and handed it to Fox.

"For you. To give you new ideas."

The pictures showed a farmer and a cat.

The farmer had chickens . . . and a problem with a fox.

The library fell silent.

Suddenly Fox slammed the book shut.

"Chiii-ckens!" he said. "Now, there's an idea!"

Mouse nodded in relief as Fox turned and ran, leaving the book on his chair.

"You're supposed to put the books back!" she called after him.

But Fox was gone.

The next night Fox was back.

"I want to take yesterday's book home with me. And you, Mouse, are coming, too. I want you to read the story to me. Because I . . . I . . . I can't read."

Mouse shook her head. "I'm sorry; I don't have time. I discovered a book of magic tricks, and I'm learning to be a magician! But the audiobooks are over there. Maybe you can find your book on a CD."

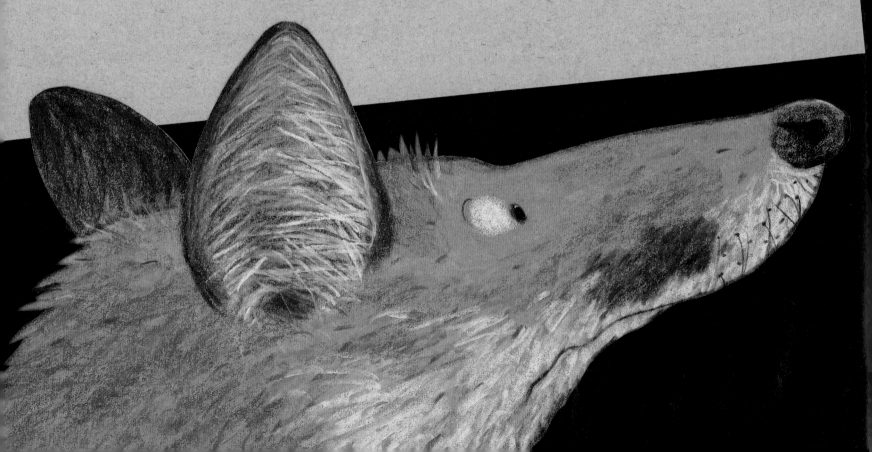

Fox was in luck!

Mouse called out to him: "You can borrow the book and the CD; just bring them back nice and clean. And don't chew anything up! You'll need a library card though and . . ."

But the book, the CD, and Fox were gone.

Three nights later Fox returned . . .

. . . with a chicken.

"What a bother! I had a chicken between my teeth when she told me that chicken bones are bad for foxes. Is that true?"

"Have a look in the encyclopedia," said Mouse, continuing to do her magic tricks.

Chicken could hardly breathe but somehow managed to read the chicken section in the encyclopedia, a pet guide, a cookbook, and Fox's storybook.

Then Fox drifted off to sleep.
Chicken drifted off to sleep, too.

Only Mouse stayed awake, practicing her magic tricks.

When the sun came up, the door opened, and people started coming into the library!

Mouse woke Chicken. Chicken woke Fox.

They started to sneak out when Chicken spotted her farmer.

She whispered to Fox, "If I went *CLUCK! CLUCK!* right now, you'd be outfoxed. Wouldn't you?"

Fox trembled. Then he narrowed his eyes and said, "Did you see what your farmer has under his arm?"

Now it was Chicken's turn to tremble.

"You know what?" said Fox. "I'll dig you a tunnel out of your chicken coop if you teach me how to read."

Chicken nodded.

They picked out a book that they both liked, then another and another. . . .

"Stop!" Mouse called out. "You can't take more than ten things out at a time! And bring them all back when they're due!"

But the books, Fox, and Chicken were gone.